W9-AGE-821

Follow the Leader

ERICA SILVERMAN

Pictures by G. BRIAN KARAS

A Sunburst Book • Farrar, Straus and Giroux

Library of Congress Cataloging-in-Publication Data
Silverman, Erica.
    Follow the leader / Erica Silverman ; pictures by G. Brian Karas. — 1st ed.
        p. cm.
    Summary: A boy guides his younger brother through a game of follow the leader—until
the little one insists on reversing roles.
    ISBN 0-374-42403-9 (pbk.)
    [1. Games—Fiction. 2. Play—Fiction. 3. Stories in rhyme.] I. Karas, G. Brian, ill.   II. Title.
PZ8.3.S58425Fo 2000
[E]—dc21
                                                                                    99-21165

To my high school English teachers,

Helen Morissey Rizzuto and Leslie Kingon. —E.S.

For David, Pilar, Adam, Alex, and Claudia. —G.B.K.

Follow the leader.
Who should it be?
I'm older. I'm bigger.
You follow me.

Follow me walking.
Hop when I hop.
Skip when I'm skipping.
Stop when I stop.

Trot like a pony.
Squat like a frog.
Leap like a rabbit over this log.

Pretend you're an eagle: flap, swoop, and land.

Turn upside down, and stand on your hands.

Yes, I'm still the leader.
Run around in a loop.
Somersault backwards.
Now hula a hoop!

Close your eyes tight.
Arms out!
Spin around!
Reach for the sky.
Drop to the ground.

Crawl to that tunnel, and follow me through.
Hey!
Don't go off that way!
Just do what I do!

March like a drummer in a parade.

Get up on this ledge. Don't be afraid.

Like an acrobat, balance. Oops! Careful, don't fall.

Next be a juggler, and juggle some balls.

Imagine we're swimming.
Dive into a pool.
But stay right behind me!
That is the rule!

Climb up the jungle gym.
Dangle. Then jump.

Sit on a swing,
and pump, pump,
pump, pump!

Step up these steps.
Ready to slide?
Don't use your hands!
Let go and glide!

No! Don't try to lead!
Not while it's my turn!
You're younger. You're smaller.
You still have to learn.

I am the leader,
and I say to freeze.
No twitching! No blinking!
Don't even sneeze!

Wait!

Why are you leaving?
You want a turn, too?
But . . .
Well . . .

Okay.
You be the leader,

and I'll follow you!